Sexy Short Stories

Hot Sex

Erotic Romance Novel for Women

Vivienne Dupont

Table of Contents

Afternoon in the café

Merle let her bike roll out and then slid off the saddle with a sweep. She briefly plucked her white summer dress with her left hand, then she leaned the bike against the lamppost, took the massive lock out of the basket and attached it. A searching jerk - everything secure. In Berlin you had to take good care of your bike, even if it was as rickety as hers.

She stroked her hands over her braided blond hair to smooth out any strands that might have been whirled up by the wind, then she took the laptop bag from the luggage rack and hung it around her neck. One last, examining pluck at her knee-length skirt before she looked left and right and ran quickly across the street towards the small Kreuzberg café "Links vom Eck", where she had been coming to work regularly for a few weeks.

At first mainly because the cupcakes were so good, but later - as she had to admit to herself with a grin - more and more because she liked one of the waiters so much.

That's why she had made herself so pretty today - because she could have answered emails in jeans and t-shirt, of course. Instead, she had chosen this airy white dress (and no bra), even though it was actually a bit too cold for the early summer temperatures. But she liked the way it played around her petite figure and accentuated her skin, which was already slightly tanned by the first summer sunrays.

A wind chime above the entrance door struck softly as she entered the café. Clattering cutlery, babble of voices and soft indie music blew towards her.

The "Links vom Eck" was well attended this afternoon (as usual at this time). It radiated the typical Berlin hipster charm, with jumbled upholstered armchairs from GDR times, golden shimmering Edison light bulbs and an absurd amount of green plants in wall shelves made of pallets between old film posters. The smell of coffee was in the air and mingled with the scent of the lime trees in front of the house that wafted in through the open window sashes.

Merle discovered Ben immediately: He was standing behind the counter, brewing a coffee by hand, moving the small silver pot of hot water in almost meditative circles. A lock of his dark hair fell into his tanned forehead, and his sharply cut nose was curled in a concentrated manner. As always he wore black jeans and a black t-shirt.

She knew that his name was Ben from the small name tag on his chest. They had never had a big conversation before.

Now he set the jug down in a sweeping movement and raised his eyes. A smile flitted across his face when he spotted Merle and briefly raised his hand in greeting.

Merle noticed her cheeks reddening slightly, but she tried not to let her joy show when she returned the silent greeting and then made her way between the tables to the last free seat at the window.

Once there, she let the bag slide off her shoulder, took out the small laptop and put it on the table. Then she sat down in the wine-red armchair, turning it so that her gaze no longer fell through the window to the outside, but into the interior of the café - and onto the counter at its rear end. She fervently hoped that this maneuver had not been too conspicuous.

The next moment, she saw Ben come out from behind the counter, grab the freshly brewed coffee and with a committed smile put it in front of a teenage girl. The little girl gave him a decidedly languishing smile, but he didn't pay any attention to her, and came across the room to Merle, pulling his waiter's pad and a pen from the pocket of his apron.

Smiling, he stopped beside her and put his head crooked. "Hey you. Same as always?"

Merle returned his smile. "Yes. And a vanilla cupcake, please."

He nodded and scribbled something on his pad, then turned back to walk. However, he gave her a quick glance and a smile over her shoulder.

Merle blushed for the second time and with a grin lowered her eyes to her laptop, which she now quickly opened to prevent herself from staring at him like a groupie.

She opened the e-mail program and clicked through a few new mails - but noticed after a few moments that she wasn't really concentrating. Her gaze flitted towards the counter as if by magic.

Ben was about to brew the rooibos tea for her, and since he was absorbed in what he was doing, she allowed herself to watch him for a moment and let her eyes wander over his muscular forearms. But then she called herself mentally to order and tried again to concentrate on her emails.

Only when she heard footsteps did she lift her gaze again. Ben stepped to her table and bent down to her to carefully place the glass with the tea next to her laptop. For a moment she had his aftershave in her nose and she almost got a little dizzy.

Her eyes fell on the cupcake, which he had now placed next to the tea.

"Oh!" Her pale blue eyes flitted up to him. "I don't think it's vanilla..."

The waiter loosely crossed his arms in front of his chest, now holding the tray loosely in his right hand.

"No, that's white chocolate passion fruit. I'm sure you'll like it better. Trust me." he winked at her briefly and then turned around again to take an order at the next table.

Merle stared at his back for a moment, then slowly stirred in her tea and looked at the cupcake. Her stomach was tingling. What was the meaning of that? Was he flirting with her?

Carefully she lifted the small tartlet and took a first small bite. The sweet fruity taste exploded in her mouth and made her close her eyes for a moment. It was really delicious!

She had already taken a second bite, then carefully wiped some butter cream off her upper lip with her index finger and licked her finger with relish.

When she opened her eyes again, she met Ben's gaze, who watched her from the other end of the room and grinned contentedly. Merle felt briefly caught, but then gave him a bright smile as she pointed briefly at the cupcake and made the thumbs-up sign.

He nodded and patted the corner of his mouth with a smile. She had missed some cream. Quickly she took the napkin and wiped it away before she turned to the rest of the cupcake.

She looked up briefly twice more and both times she met Ben's gaze. She thought she could feel him almost physically, even when she wasn't looking. But she forced herself not to look over to him a third time.

For the next two hours, Merle actually worked quite concentrated. But finally she felt her attention fade and her gaze again rushed over to the waiter more often.

Determined, she closed the laptop and stretched for a moment. Enough for today.

She got up and went over to the toilets. Of course she passed the counter and Ben again. Once again they exchanged a smile.

While she washed her hands in the small bathroom shortly thereafter, Merle feverishly thought about how she could possibly involve the waiter in a longer conversation. But everything she could think of sounded clumsy and boring in her ears. Maybe next time.

With a sigh she opened the toilet door to step out into the hallway - and almost collided with Ben, who was apparently on his way back to the kitchen with a stack of empty plates.

"Oops", he laughed and just about caught the top two plates that had started to slip due to his quick evasive movement.

Merle's heart, however, had made a frightened leap. "Oh, sorry! Everything go all right?"

Ben nodded and put his head slightly crooked. "Do you want to go home?"

She shrugged her bare shoulders. "Yeah, it's about time. My concentration is gone." A helpless grin.

He seemed to hesitate for a moment, threw a prudent glance down the short hallway into the guest room, and then, with a conspiratorial grin, grabbed her left hand. "Come with me a moment."

Merle, far too baffled to resist (if she had wanted to resist at all), was dragged two steps down the aisle and then through a wooden swinging door into the small café kitchen.

Clanking, Ben placed the stack of plates on the stainless steel counter and then turned to the little man with a semi bald head and oversized white apron, who was just about to wipe the counter and now looked up irritated.

"Hey, Manni, can you watch the front for a second?"

The one so addressed drew his bushy eyebrows together in consternation, glanced briefly back and forth between Ben and Merle, but then straightened up and with a sigh dropped the tea towel.

"If I have to..." He shuffled slowly past them both and out of the kitchen.

The kitchen in which Merle suddenly found herself alone with Ben was not very big, but it was stuffed to the ceiling with cupboards and shelves. Two large refrigerators hummed quietly in one corner and from a large oven there was a tempting smell of cheesecake.

At the edge of the counter, which Manni had just cleaned, half a dozen bowls and piping bags piled up with leftover buttercream and frosting, as well as the dishes that Ben had carelessly unloaded there. But now he turned back to Merle and grinned at her crookedly.

"Sorry for the ambush... but since you were just leaving, I had to take my chance..." The look of his dark eyes went through Merle.

She suddenly realized that it was the first time she had been alone with him. Nevertheless, she still did not quite understand the situation. Although... well, that had to mean that he was interested in her, right? Unless he just wanted to know the brand of her laptop or something. But he didn't have to drag her into the kitchen for that. Did he?

Merle smiled insecurely and shoved a strand of hair behind his ear. "Um, no problem, so..."

But then he already interrupted her. "Well, since you liked the cupcake so much, I thought you might want a refill." He leaned back against the counter and reached for one of the bowls. Shoulder shrug. "They'll throw it away."

With a grin he held the small bowl out to her and Merle recognized the passion fruit frosting from her cupcake.

She laughed brightly and accepted them. "Oh, sure!"

A short reassuring look at him - he nodded invitingly - then she dipped her index finger into the small remainder of cream, put it in her mouth and licked it off with relish. Pure, the butter cream was once again a whole lot more fruity. She immediately took a second portion.

Meanwhile Ben had watched her contentedly and grinned now when it tasted so obvious to her. He himself took a bowl of dark brown frosting and put a finger of it in his mouth.

"I'm more of a chocolate fan myself."

Merle, now almost a little brave, took a step towards him. "Oh, chocolate's good too..."

When he held the bowl out to her, she took a finger full of it and put it between her full lips.

This time she took a little more time for licking: Slowly she let her index finger slide through her closed lips and held Ben's gaze the whole time. Even though it was hard for her, because in the meantime a whole horde of nervous butterflies fluttered in her stomach.

Ben's smile became wider. He did not let her out of his sight. His voice had become a little quieter now that she was standing right in front of him.

"You seem to like it..."

He grabbed one of the remaining piping bags from the counter and turned it over in his muscular hands while examining it. "I think that's whiskey-caramel. Fancy a little kick?" With a wry grin he lifted his eyes back to Merle.

She probably wouldn't have said no if it had simply been vanilla.
She nodded. "Sure..."

Ben straightened up and took the last remaining half step towards her. "Okay, open your mouth."

Merle's heart beat up to her throat, but she hesitated only a tiny moment, then she opened her lips.

He lightly grasped her chin with his left hand, then he carefully injected a splash of frosting into her mouth with his right hand.

Merle, her eyes fixed on him, almost automatically closed his mouth and swallowed. But she hardly noticed what she was tasting. She was too distracted by the touch of his fingers on her jaw and his smell, which now enveloped her completely.

Perhaps he looked at her state of mind, or at least he smiled knowing that he knew it for a moment. Then he lifted the bag questioningly.

She nodded slightly and opened her mouth again.

Again he squirted a small portion onto her tongue. But this time she had hardly swallowed when she suddenly felt his lips on hers.

Scared, she drew in the air, but then she already felt his hand push into her neck and the next moment she was already nestling up against his chest.

It tasted like chocolate and a little bit like cigarettes. His lips were full and soft, but at the same time demanding and pressing.

Already his tongue was pushed between her lips and she opened them without resistance, at the same time wrapping her left arm around his neck - in her right hand she was still holding the bowl with the passion fruit frosting.

The next moment she felt him carefully take the bowl out of her hand and push it carelessly behind her on the counter. His tongue stroked her lower lip.
Then his hands grasped her waist, turned her without interrupting the kiss, and for a moment she felt the edge of the metal counter at her hip. But already he grabbed her tighter, lifted her up with a jerk and placed her on the work surface.

Merle gasped in surprise, lost contact with his lips for a moment - but before she could open her eyes, he was already near, pushed himself between her thighs and kissed her again.

His hands stroked across her back, along her spine, while she herself buried her fingers in his dark curls - and for a tiny moment worried that she was smearing butter cream in his hair.

The very next moment this thought was wiped away, for his lips were now separated from hers, wandering across her cheek, along her jaw, then across her neck.

Merle shivered, let his head sink into the neck.

Ben kissed the spot under her earlobe, at the same time his hands slid up her back, over her naked shoulder blades and to the straps of her dress. He murmured a soft, almost a little rough: "You taste so good..."

Then he gently - but emphatically - pushed the straps of her dress over her shoulders and further down her upper arms.

Merle shuddered as the rough linen cloth stroked over her naked skin. The neckline of the dress was wide, yet it stuck briefly to her breasts.

Ben deftly opened the two buttons at the neckline of her dress with his fingers and it slid down to her hips, exposing the gently tanned hills of her bare breasts. Her nipples contracted hard.

The waiter moaned with a suppressed groan, stroking with his right hand from her décolleté between her breasts and over her flat stomach.

Merle trembled. Released his hands from the straps of the slipped down dress and let them slide tremblingly over her chest and shoulders. For a moment, their eyes met and she became even more dizzy from the eager sparkle in his eyes.

Then Ben suddenly grinned again and reached for another piping bag - this time without paying much attention to what kind of frosting was in it. Instead of squirting the cream into Merle's mouth, he now squirted it in a short line on her décolleté, bent down the next moment and licked the cream off her soft skin with his tongue.

Merle sighed shudderingly and clawed his hands lightly into his shirt.

Again he pulled out the bag, under gentle pressure the pale yellow cream now swelled on her left breast, just covering her hard nipple.

She felt the sticky heaviness of the cream, then again his lips, his tongue, slower this time.

Her hands slipped into his neck as his lips closed around her nipple, a groan escaped her mouth - quickly biting her lower lip.

He briefly sucked on her bud, then let the tip of his tongue slowly circle around it, carefully licking up the last bit of cream.

Merle's breath started trembling, her head had sunk into her neck, her eyes closed. She pressed her back slightly to bend towards him and his caressing tongue. She already felt another drop of frosting on her skin - this time on her right breast.

His mouth followed no heartbeat later, more pressing now - hungrier. He licked up the cream and once again played around her hard nipple, chasing hot waves through Merle's body. It became harder and harder for her to keep still, her breath became more hectic -

quickly the sticky, smeared hills of her breasts rose and fell.

Suddenly, however, a loud door slam and an incredulous "Dude, you're serious! "
Merle flinched violently and opened her blue eyes. Over Ben's shoulder she saw Manni standing in the doorway, her hands on her hips, her eyebrows now drawn together so that they almost touched.

Ben had also stood up jerkily and spun around to the door, while Merle hastily tried to pull the slipping dress back over her smudged breasts.

"Manni!"

But there the cook had already turned around with a "Mmpf" and pulled back through the violently swinging kitchen door into the aisle.

Ben turned to the blushing Merle, stroked her cheek with his right hand and with his thumb briefly over her full lower lip.

A whispered "Don't move," then he turned around, tugged his shirt up as he walked, and the next moment he was gone out into the hallway.

Merle, however, remained in complete shock for a moment, then her heart slowly began to beat more regularly again and she looked down in surprise. With her left hand she still pressed the white cloth of her dress against her bare breasts, even though she now noticed that she had covered them more badly than right.

Frosting remains and saliva glittered on her skin. Left and right of her were piping bags and bowls, two of them tipped over.

Her lap was throbbing.

Through the door she heard soft but fast voices.

Oh my God, what was she doing here?

Carefully she tried to unravel the top of the dress, but then the kitchen door rattled again and her blue look shot up in shock.

But it was only Ben, who pushed himself back into the kitchen with a boyish grin and brushed the dark hair out of his forehead. But when he noticed that Merle was about to put her clothes back on, he took two quick steps and effortlessly caught her hands with his own.

Already he pushed himself between her thighs again and Merle felt his lips glide over her neck. "Oh, no..." His voice was a calming and at the same time hungry murmur.

He pulled his hands from her chest and after a moment of hesitation she let it happen and let go of the dress. Rustling, the cloth slid back to her hips.

With a muttered "Where were we...?" his lips lay on hers again and he kissed her greedily.

Merle wrestled with herself for a moment, even bringing out an incoherent "Ben...but...Manni...", but then the renewed flare-up of excitement soon drove every thought out of her head. Her eyelids sank down.

When he separated from her a few heartbeats later, she was long since a breathless bundle of quivering excitement.

"Open..."

She heard his voice only as if through thick fog, but obeyed instantly, even though she kept her eyes closed. Already she tasted strawberry... or raspberry...? She sucked greedily on the piping bag he had put between her lips.

She heard him laugh softly, then felt his lips again on her breasts, the left one, a nibble, a bite - she groaned.

Buried his hands in his hair again. Frosting smacked her chin, then she heard a thud, he must have dropped the bag.

She felt his hands on her hips and his lips on her mouth again. Tasted strawberry and him, greedily opened his lips for his tongue.

Barely noticing how he pushed up the skirt of her dress, shuddering only under his hands, which slid over her bare thighs and pushed them a little further apart.

A quiet ratchet, then his hand between her legs, his fingers pulling aside the long since wet fabric of her panties.

Merle flinched under the touch, gasped at his lips, but instead of backing away she wrapped her bare legs around his hips.

In the next moment she felt his hard cock pressing against her hot throbbing vulva, pushing past the fabric of her panties and without hesitation parting her swollen labia.

She groaned as he penetrated her completely, stretched her and filled her up.

Her hands clawed harder into Ben's curls, her moans could no longer be suppressed by his mouth.

She barely felt him grab her hips, pull her tighter, penetrate her even deeper. Just felt how he moved inside her and began to fuck her with quick thrusts.

Panting, she reared up in his arms, pulled him tighter and tighter, writhing, wanting to feel him even closer, even deeper. Her bare breasts rubbed against the fabric of his shirt, the hard buds tickling.

As he released the kiss, she gasped for breath. She dropped her head to the neck, gasped, groaned.

He fucked her faster, harder. Pushed her backwards, halfway down the counter.

She tried to brace herself and accidentally wiped a bowl off the counter, which broke clinking. Hearing his gasped "Never mind..." at her neck, she felt his hand, which now clasped her left breast and kneaded greedily.

Merle reared up to meet him - he just pushed her harder. Faster.

"Oh yeah...yeah..." Her wheezing was a plea, she had long since stopped caring if you could hear her outside the kitchen (and you probably could).

She only felt the sizzling heat in her body, his hard cock filling her, his fingers kneading her chest.

Her skin now glistened not only from frosting but also from sweat.
"Harder..." she whimpered between two moaned breaths.

She heard now also his loud wheezing, tugged at his shirt, clung to his neck with one hand.

One more push, one more and one more.

The muscles in her abdomen began to tense up, as did her toes in the leather sandals. The climax grabbed her with fiery force, hurled her head into her neck and tore a tortured outcry from her.

She twitched and fidgeted under him, panting and screaming.

Ben grabbed her tighter, now also panting violently, pushed one last time into her pulsating abdomen and poured himself out with a loud groan.

Merle felt his cock twitching and pumping inside her, while the raging waves of her own orgasm almost robbed her of her senses.

Trembling and gasping for breath, she collapsed on the work counter, felt him bending over her, breathing heavily, his hands resting next to her.

While the waves of her own climax ebbed only slowly, he pulled his tail out of her, panting.

His juice ran sticky over the inside of her thigh.

When Merle finally got her breath back, she opened her blue eyes and blinked slightly disorientated into the bright neon light.

Ben grinned at her, then helped her to stand up and pull her dress back up. She was still trembling, struggling to pull the fabric over her stained breasts and her arms through the taped straps.

Breathing heavily, Ben leaned next to her at the bar, first stroking himself and then her hair from her face. He grinned at her and Merle replied uncertainly and still shaky.

Slipped off the work counter, stumbled briefly and was grateful that he grabbed her by the elbow while supporting her. She adjusted her dress and then blinked up to him.

"I... I should... wanted... leave..." She grinned.

He nodded with a smile, but then quickly bent over to a shelf and took a freshly baked cupcake from its mould. With a sweeping movement he squirted the last bit of strawberry (or raspberry) cream on it and held it out to her with a grin.

"To go? - This one's on me. "

The photoshoot

Charlotte fled at the last moment before the onset of rain and scurried into the entrance of the house. This morning she had spent almost an hour at her trusted hairdresser's and had had her red-blond mane elaborately shaped into luxurious curls. She would really have hated to have it ruined by the rain.

All in all, she had dressed up unusually elaborately today: To high-heeled black pumps with voluminous bows at the sides she wore a short black cocktail dress that fabulously emphasized her curves. Underneath was the underwear she had bought especially for the occasion. Even though she felt a little bit dressed up, she felt at the same time how the exquisite wardrobe changed her attitude and charisma.

Her gaze glided over the bell plates and soon she discovered what she was looking for:

B. Matuschek
Photographer

With a nervously fluttering stomach Charlotte pressed the bell button and almost at the same moment the front door gave way to her pressure with a buzzing sound.

She entered a typical, slightly run-down Kreuzberg stairwell. Graffiti on the rusty mailboxes in the corner, the old-fashioned stair railing painted over many times. The plaster crumbled from the high ceiling. There was a small café on the first floor of the house and the smell of coffee and pastries followed Charlotte up to the second floor.

There, in the wide open door to the left, the man she had an appointment with was already leaning against the wall: Bernd Matuschek, photographer. He was in his mid-forties, with thick black hair and a sinewy figure. A little bit taller than her, even with the high-heeled pumps.

With a friendly smile he extended his hand to her. "Hello, you must be Charlotte?"

Charlotte blinked and felt how she blushed slightly - for a moment the nervousness in her head rushed. Then she regained her composure and cleared her throat.

"Yes... yes, I am. We spoke on the telephone, Mr. Matuschek" Her voice sounded a little rough. She cleared her throat again.

The person addressed nodded and stepped aside to let them enter with an inviting movement. "I hope you found it good. It's a bit hidden."

"Yes, I know... I've been to the cafe downstairs many times."

"Oh, yeah, that hipster place." He sighed briefly, but then grinned apologetically as he closed the door behind them. "No offense."

The apartment, which was converted into a photo studio, was sparsely furnished: in the hallway only a narrow bench under a series of large-format black-and-white photographs. On the right a small kitchen, and at the end of the hallway the largest room.

High white walls, on one of which the plaster was removed and the rough masonry was exposed. In front of it was a large, dark brown leather couch. The large window front faced the courtyard - one wing was open and the sound of the rushing rain filled the whole apartment. Spotlights, tripods, and a table with a computer and two monitors completed the professional ambience.

Charlotte's pumps clacked on the polished floorboards as she followed the photographer into the room.

"You want to take pictures for your husband, right?" Invitingly, he pointed to the leather couch and then, when she had sat down, sat down at a proper distance on a squeaking swivel stool.

Charlotte nodded and laid her coat, which she had worn over her arm, on the back of the sofa. "Yes...

exactly. It should be a surprise for him. So... they should be erotic photos." She blushed - nonsensically, because they had already discussed this in advance.

Mr. Matuschek smiled, just as friendly as professional. "Exactly. A beautiful idea. I often have customers who want erotic pictures."

"Oh - really?" Charlotte looked up in surprise.

Almost apologetically he raised his hands and grinned. "It can be very stimulating for the partnership ..."

Charlotte nodded, then lowered her eyes for a moment. "Yes... I've had the impression lately that my husband doesn't look at me properly..."

"I can hardly imagine that, with a beauty like you."

The photographer smiled, but Charlotte waved a mocking little laugh. "What else can you say now..." Then she became more serious again. "No, he's surrounded by such pretty young things at work every day." For a moment she looked at the photographer thoughtfully, but then - again with a smile - she quickly continued. "Anyway, I hope he sees me in a new light through the photos."

Mr. Matuschek nodded. "We should succeed." His smile was as winning as it was reassuring.

He pointed down the hall. "Would you like to freshen up in the bathroom? In the meantime, I'll prepare everything here and then we can get started."

When Charlotte came back, the photographer had moved the sofa a little away from the wall, turned on two spotlights and put on soft jazz music. Now he was fiddling around with a camera, but looked up when she stepped into the room.

"Adorable."

Charlotte blushed slightly again and waved away. At the same time she could not hide the fact that the compliment did her good. She hadn't really done much, just freshened up her makeup, applied a new layer of rust-red lipstick and a few splashes of perfume and tidied up her black dress. Still, she felt completely different than usual. Femme fatale instead of housewife and mother.

Mr. Matuschek pointed to the sofa, while he himself reached for a bottle of champagne and held it up questioningly. "Would you like a sip? Just to relax?" He grinned.

Charlotte hesitated briefly, but then she nodded with a smile. "Yes, maybe that's a good idea."

He poured her a drink and shortly afterwards she found herself on the cool cushion of the sofa with a champagne glass in her hand. Nervously she took a sip, pleasantly tingling, the alcohol ran down her throat. She felt how she relaxed a little.

Meanwhile, the photographer had adjusted one of the headlights and then positioned himself behind his camera. "We will start with a few normal shots. To warm up..." He smiled at her across the camera and Charlotte nodded.

At first she was irritated by the clicking of the camera, she felt awkward and wooden, even had difficulties to make a smile.

But after only a few minutes she began to relax - or maybe it was simply the champagne that slowly began to show its effect. For the first few shots she had simply sat in the middle of the sofa with her legs crossed, but now - following the photographer's instructions - she began to move more.

She tilted her head, turned to the side. She stretched out an arm, supported herself, put it on the back of the sofa. Turned her head in profile.

"Yes!

Click Click.

"Very nice."

Click.

"Just like that."

His enthusiastic reception ran through Charlotte's body as tingling as the champagne. She could not remember the last time she had felt so beautiful. The silky fabric of the dress rustled softly with each of her movements, gliding pleasantly cool over her skin. The leather of the sofa creaked. The smell of her perfume and the hairspray in her curls made her dizzy.

Click Click.

Another sip of champagne. Over the edge of the glass she looked over to the camera, her eyelids half lowered, her long eyelashes darkly mascaraed.

Click Click.

The photographer moved a little closer with his camera.

Although he did not look at her directly, but at the camera's display, she had never felt so intensely observed in her life.

Click.

Charlotte became more courageous now, needed his instructions less and less. She leaned back, pushed her back through. One hand went through the red curls, closed her eyes for a moment, opened her made-up lips.

Click Click.

She looked up again, looked at him, took another sip. Then put the glass on the floor in front of her feet. She stood up again, her stocked leg reaching up with the fingertips of her right hand, light as a feather.

Click Click.

Slowly she raised her hand to her shoulder, pushed it under the thin strap of her dress and let it slide over her shoulder. Looking into the camera from below.

"Wonderful..."

Was it her imagination, or had his voice become a little rougher?

She let the second pose follow, briefly crossed her arms in front of her full breasts, pressed them up, milky and beautifully swollen, revealed from the now slipped down neckline of her dress.

Click Click.

He came two steps closer.

Charlotte stood up, turned around and turned her back on him. Reached back and with a quiet ratchet, pulled down the short zipper of her dress. Then, in a single rustling movement, let the dress slide off her body.

The ubiquitous clicking stopped and she clearly heard him sucking in the air behind her in surprise.

She wore a black lace thong, black stockings and matching suspenders, plus a corsage that left her breasts free and merely pushed them upwards. Never before had she worn anything even remotely wicked.

Click Click.

Charlotte looked over her shoulder into the camera, pushed the red curls over her shoulder and bathed in the frantic clicking of the camera. She turned slightly, the full mounds of her breasts now in profile, her nipples hard contracted by the cool air from the window.

The photographer, now silenced, did not seem to want to let go of the shutter release of his camera. With slow movements he walked around her in a semicircle, photographing her from all sides.

Charlotte let herself slide back onto the sofa, enjoying the cool leather on her noticeably heated skin. It creaked when she leaned back, and she let her upper body slide onto the seat.

Click Click.

Matuschek stood not half a step away from her, looking down at her through the black eye of the camera. She lounged, stretched.

He nodded, and she sensed a little nervousness. "Very... nice..." His voice was soft and yes - clearly rougher.

Charlotte ran her fingertips along her collarbone, pushed the curls aside and down onto the leather seat. Then let her fingertips move deeper, across the arch of her chest.

Click Click.

She closed her eyes. Slowly encircled the hard buds.

Click.

Rubbed over them again. A sigh bubbled from her slightly open red lips. Blushing, she opened her eyes, looked up at him.

But the photographer seemed to be spellbound by her and murmured softly: "Wonderful...".

He now kneeled with one leg on the seat of the sofa, not two centimeters from her legs. Again, he pressed the shutter button. "Keep going..."

Charlotte rubbed again over her left nipple.

"Yes..." muttered the photographer.

His captured attention made them more self-confident - more courageous. She now also took her right hand and closed it around her other breast. Pressed her hand into the light-colored flesh, massaging almost agonisingly slowly. Meanwhile she continued to play with her left nipple, rubbing it between thumb and index finger and pulling it a little long.

Click Click.

She felt how her centre began to glow more and more, how the touches - but even more the constant clicking of the camera - excited her. And the attention of the photographer, who circled around her like a rare animal.

Since he had got up from the sofa again, she now used the space and spread her thighs. Let her right foot slide from the seat to the floor. Squeezed his back and closed his eyes for a moment.

Click Click.

The right hand, still clawed into her chest, slid down her left, stroking the firm fabric of the lace-trimmed corsage that tightly gripped her centre. Her breaths had become shallower - shallower and faster. The tightness of the corsage made it a little difficult for her to breathe, but the feeling was not unpleasant.

Her fingers reached her thigh, stroking down and - further inside - up again.

The photographer took a few steps back.

Click Click.

Then came closer again.

Charlotte spread her legs a little more. She blinked, looking for the eye of the camera. Matuschek had now positioned herself behind her head, taking pictures, so to speak, along her stretched out body. Charlotte could hear him breathing. Fast and deep. His excitement only inflamed hers even more.

Click Click.

Fully aware that the movement from his perspective could not escape him, she slipped her fingers between her thighs, over the wafer-thin fabric of her panties.

An involuntary moaning.

Was it him or her?

She rubbed across her middle, feeling the dampness that had begun to soak the fabric. Warm waves chased her body upwards.

Then she looked up. "Would you like to see pictures like these, Mr. Matuschek?" Her voice seemed strange to her, darker and velvety than usual.

The clicking stopped again.

She pressed her pelvis against her hand, pressed the ball of her hand against the mound of Venus.

"Yes... yes... who, well who wouldn't like that..."

Click.

"Do you like me?" She twirled her right nipple between her fingers. Sweet, arousing pain.

Click Click.

"Yes...of course!"

"Would you like to touch me, Mr. Matuschek"

Again the clicking stopped for a short time.

His voice sounded pressed. "That would be - hardly appropriate..."

The effect she had on him was astounding.

He walked along the back of the sofa and to its other end.

Charlotte followed him with her gaze. Angled her left leg, which had been lying on the seat of the couch, and put her foot on the backrest.

The photographer drew the air in sharply - the camera's focus remained for a moment on its now invitingly presented centre.

Click Click.

Charlotte bit her lower lip. "Yes... hardly appropriate." She slowly and agonisingly pushed the index and middle finger of her left hand *under* the fabric of her panties. "You can't just pick on your... customers..."

Click.

He shakes his head. "No, that would be very..."

Under the transparent fabric of the panties, Charlotte's fingers shared her freshly shaved labia, stroking slowly down between them. She moaned.

Her eyelids fluttered, but she still noticed that the knuckles on the photographer's hands were white - that's how tightly he clasped his camera. It turned her on how much she turned him on.

Click Click.

With slippery fingertips she began to orbit her clitoris. Her pelvis twitched. Her full breasts trembled under her increasingly rapid breaths.

Click.

"But would you like...?" Her voice trembled with excitement.

The photographer came closer, now between her spread thighs, again with one knee on the seat. Her knee touched his side.

He photographed her breasts, her hand, which now almost clawed into the soft curve, looking for a hold. The excitement in her face. The half open lips and half closed eyes. Her centre was pressed together by the corsage. The hand in her panties, the fingers rubbing her sensitive pearl faster and faster.

Click Click Click Click.

Charlotte could see the drops of sweat on his forehead.

Her question remained unanswered, but the bulge in his pants spoke volumes.

She closed her eyes and let her head sink into the neck. Increased the pressure with which she played around her clitoris. "I think..." Shortly, she penetrated with her fingers inside herself, and bit herself on the lip in order to suppress a groan.

She blinked back up to him and the camera. "I think... you'd like to..." The rest of the movement passed in another groan as she rubbed again - now faster - over her pearl.

"Don't stop..." was his only answer. That and the frantic clicking of the camera.

Charlotte moaned. Lolling - writhing. She rubbed faster. Loosened her right hand from her chest, clawed her briefly in her red curls, then pressed her against the side of the couch from below. Her muscles tightened. The excitement in her lap became more and more pressing, more and more hungry.

Click Click.

Her foot slipped off the back of the couch, knees and thighs fell against the photographer's side, but he didn't back off. Instead, he bent over her just a little further.

Click Click Click.

Charlotte blinked, struggling to keep her eyes open. She wanted to see him, wanted to see the camera. The camera that captured her every move.

Moaning, she pressed the pelvis against her hand, rubbing her clitoris harder and harder. Feeling her muscles begin to contract painfully, the first waves of the climax seized her.

"Yes... go on..." He almost gasped it.

Click Click.

Matuschek photographed her face, distorted by excitement. Her billowing breasts. The wet shimmering centre.

Panting, Charlotte bent her back, reared up. Glaring red waves robbed her of her view for a moment, everything seemed to turn.

Click.

Her thigh pressed against his side, her pelvis twitched in rhythmic contractions.

Click Click.

Moaning, she threw her head back into the neck.

Click.

Finally, finally, Charlotte's finger came to rest. Gasping for breath, she slumped heavily down onto the leather upholstery of the couch. Opened her eyes. Her body was swirling hot and bright and sensual.

With a sigh she sat up, her face now suddenly less than five centimetres away from the camera lens.

The photographer retreated, leaning against the side rest of the sofa. His eyes shimmered darkly, his breath went shallow. For the moment, the clicking of the camera was silenced.

Charlotte supported herself with her hands between her spread legs, bending slightly forward. The upper arms pressed her bare breasts together. Still her body trembled from the last waves of the climax.

She looked up at him. "Did you like that, Mr. Matuschek?"

The person addressed had let the camera sink, looked at her as demandingly as impatiently. "You can see it clearly..."

Charlotte laughed softly, cooing. Her power over him was intoxicating.

She straightened up a little further, now kneeling on the seat of the sofa. Her right hand touched his knee, stroking up his thigh over the fabric of his jeans. Meanwhile her green gaze remained lifted to him motionless. Fascinated, she watched him swallow, his muscles trembling under the tension.

For a moment she considered stopping, letting him stew, torturing him. To remain a good and faithful housewife. But the temptation was too great.

Her fingers reached his hip - briefly rubbing her palm over the bump in his pants, he groaned. Charlotte smiled. Seeing how much he wanted her made her lose all inhibitions. There was no more room for shame or doubt. Her fingers closed around his belt.

With an almost agonised groan, he slipped off the side of the sofa, but not to escape it - instead, he stopped right in front of the sofa (and thus in front of her).

Loosened one hand from the camera and slid it under the tousled curls in her neck.

Charlotte unbuckled his belt with deft fingers, then his pants. His hard cock literally jumped towards her.

He moaned.

She closed her fingers around him, still slippery wet from her own juice. Stroking up and down the shaft. Bent forward and opened the red shimmering lips.

He let go of her neck, grabbed the camera again.

Click click.

She looked up to him while her tongue carefully touched the tip of his tail, slowly sliding around her.

Panting, he gasped for air. His tail became even a little harder.

Charlotte opened her mouth wider, let it slowly slide in and closed her red lips around the shaft.

Click.

The camera tracked her every move, even if the photographer's hands were shaking so much that she doubted whether the images were particularly sharp.

"What would... your husband say..." The photographer's rough voice sounded as tortured as it did greedy.

Click Click.

Charlotte - his cock deep in her mouth - paused briefly. Then she let it slowly slide out again, stroking with her tongue over the underside. "He has... had his chance... or...?"

His tail shimmered wet from her saliva, a little red from the lipstick. She sucked slightly at the tip.

"Idiot..." The photographer gasped for breath. His pelvis twitched.

Charlotte nodded, then let his cock slide back into her mouth. Started sucking it. He moaned.

Click Click.

Her hands now lay on his hip, her fingers clawed at his belt.

Click.

Her bare breasts rubbed against the rough fabric of his jeans, tingling waves spread from her hard nipples through her still lustfully throbbing body.

Click Click.

She spread her knees, the leather of the sofa creaked. Her glowing center shimmered moistly under the lace fabric of the thong.

Click.

With her tongue she played around his hard cock, let it slide in and out of her mouth again and again.

Faster.

He wheezed.

Suddenly a sound that she could not place, then his hands that grabbed her head. He had thrown the camera onto the sofa.

Charlotte moaned as his hands clawed into her curls.

She only sucked even harder.

He grabbed her tighter, began to direct her head, fuck her mouth. She let it happen, fitted into his movements, his rhythm.

The photographer's greed, which until then had been so laboriously controlled, finally broke its course.

Hart pushed his tail into her mouth, pressed deep into her throat.

Charlotte gasped, had to gag.

He moaned. Pressed her on his pelvis, pushed her head away again, only to ram his cock into her throat again the next moment.

Charlotte's hands clasped his wrists, but rather seeking a hold than resisting. The fire in her lap flared up a second time, hot and consuming.

Over and over again she had to choke - but noticed that exactly this seemed to excite him even more.

Moaning, she pressed herself against his legs.

Never had her husband ever treated her in such a way, so demanding, so greedy, so completely obsessed with possessing her.

She tore herself away from him, took away her mouth.

Matuschek cursed.

Charlotte, however, clawed her hands into the fabric of his shirt, pulled herself up against it until she was balancing on the sofa in pumps. In a single movement she had grabbed her panties, pulled them over her bottom and carelessly let them fall down to her ankles.

She wanted him, all the way.

Charlotte grabbed the photographer's shoulders and the next moment he landed next to her in the cushions.

She sank astride on his lap. She felt his hard cock, which pressed greedily against her shaved pussy.

She moved her pelvis.

The photographer moaned.

Charlotte shoved her hands into his neck, rubbing his cock more urgently.

He wheezed. His tail found its way as if by itself, the tip already squeezed into her slippery opening.

She sighed, tilted the pelvis and let him enter completely.

Matushek's hands clawed into her naked bottom. He moaned.

Charlotte began to move her pelvis, riding him with slow movements. His tail slid in and out, again and again, fanning the fire in her pelvis.

Her head sank into the neck, the red curls poured out in dishevelled cascades over her swaying breasts.

His hand moved up her back, his lips found her breasts, closed around one of the buds. He sucked on it.

Charlotte moaned. Her movements became faster.

"Oh yeah...", the photographer gasped at her breast. He writhed under her. Now she was the one who forced her rhythm on him.

Whenever she felt his tail twitching inside her, she paused. Let him curse tortured and claw his hands into her bottom. Then she moved again, rode him hard and fast, felt him almost coming again - and stopped again.

The control intoxicated her, her own excitement glowing in every fibre of her body. To feel him wriggling under her almost made her come.

Faster and faster she moved her pelvis, deeper and deeper became her moaning.

Her eyes had long since closed, her hands clawed into his shoulders.

His tongue, his lips glided breathlessly, unsupported over her skin - her shoulders, her breasts, her neck.

"Charlotte," he moaned in agony.

She came. For the second time. And much more violently.

Screaming, she threw her head back into the neck.

Her hands threatened to rip his shirt to shreds.

The muscles in her abdomen contracted, closing tightly around his tail.

With a groan he came there too, poured out pulsating and wheezing deep inside her body.

Charlotte twitched, threw herself back and forth in his arms.

Then - finally - collapsed moaning above him. Her head sank against his shoulder.

Her breath fluttered. Everything in her glowed.

His hands stroked her back, first uncontrollably, then more and more slowly. More lovingly.

She still felt his tail in her body, slowly getting limper.

With a sigh her fluttering eyelids lifted. She met his dark gaze.

His fingertips caressed her neck. He smiled, satisfied and impressed. Breathed a kiss on her lips and then mumbled: "That was so much hornier than I had expected, honey...".

A Tinder Date full of surprises

Katharina was a little nervous when she got off the bus and tried to find her way around this part of Kreuzberg. Sam had suggested the café "Links vom Eck" as a meeting place and had also written her which stop she had to get off at to find it. So it should not be too far away.

During the ride she had briefly called up Sam's Tinder profile again: He had uploaded only one picture and that showed him diagonally in his profile. Finely cut, almost androgynous features and soft dark brown hair that fell into his eyes. He also wore expensive looking black headphones in the photo.
These were then also the starting point for their conversation: Katharina had learned that music was Sam's passion. He also originally came from the USA, but had lived in Berlin for almost ten years and worked in a tech company.

This was by no means Katharina's first Tinder-Date - lately she was really eager to find the big love - but still she got quite nervous before. It was just strange to suddenly find yourself face to face with someone you only knew the photo and maybe a few WhatsApp lines from before.

Katharina turned left and began walking down the street lined with lime trees. She hadn't dressed up much and was wearing a short-sleeved white blouse with dark jeans that accentuated her lush curves. Her long black hair fell openly over her shoulders and framed her heart-shaped face. Her only makeup was a cherry red lipstick.

To her relief, a few metres away she actually spotted the sign of the café she was looking for and took a look at her slim wristwatch: she was even a little early. She briefly considered whether she should go inside, but then decided to wait outside. She quickly wrote a message to Sam that she had arrived - then she leaned against a small wall on the right side of the café and let her eyes wander across the street.

She hated this moment when people looked for the only vaguely known other, thought they recognised them in every second passer-by, and then smiled unsure and a bit stupidly at strangers - uncertainly judging whether they showed any sign of recognition.

As the minutes passed, Katharina became more and more nervous. She checked her cell phone twice, but hadn't received a message from Sam. Did he stand her up?

In the next moment she was almost knocked down by a cyclist who made an emergency stop less than half a metre in front of her and jumped off his bike.

"Katharina?"

Her eyes almost fell out of her head. At the same time the redness shot into her pale cheeks. In front of her stood Sam: the brown hair, the high cheekbones, even the headphones, which lay around her narrow neck like a collar. But just as clearly, Sam was a *woman*.

Katharina blinked, too perplexed for a moment to say anything.

Sam, too, now seemed a little confused - probably because of Katharina's shocked expression - and tilted her head questioningly. "You are Katharina, aren't you?" Then she reached out her hand. "I am Sam."

Katharina now at least managed to take the hand she was offered. "Hi...yes...I am Katharina. Hi." But then she still shook her head irritated. "Sorry I am... this is now..."

How the hell did that happen? You had set your search filter to men, didn't you? Had Sam posed as a man? On the other hand, she had been shown pictures of women every now and then - she didn't know exactly why. She had simply ignored them.

Sam now seemed seriously worried, her eyebrows slightly raised above the large amber eyes. "Is everything all right with you?" She pointed to the wheel. "Did I scare you? I'm sorry."

Hastily Katharina shook her head. "No." And then burst out: "I thought you were a man..."

Sam opened her eyes. "What?!" For a moment she didn't seem to know whether to be horrified or amused - then a gurgling little laugh escaped her throat.

"Seriously? But my profile clearly says 'female'..."

The grin made her whole face glow, at the same time she had pulled her eyebrows together in comical desperation.

Katharina - who at the moment could not laugh at all about this extremely embarrassing situation - reached for her cell phone, even though she knew that she was behaving insanely rudely. She had already opened Sam's profile, scrolled down and there it was. She stared at the display in amazement. How could she have missed that? Well, she usually didn't pay much attention to the profile texts, but based her selection on the photos alone, but at least after the match she would have...

Sam's bright voice tore her from her thought carousel. "Well that's a first..." Then she shrugged her shoulders, apparently already over the first shock that Katharina still had to struggle with. "Would you like to have a coffee anyway? Now that we are here already?" She pointed invitingly to the café.

Katharina looked helplessly back and forth between Sam and the front door. She would have liked best to sink into the ground in shame. But that was really not an option. And to leave Sam standing here seemed to her to be more than mean - especially since the whole thing had obviously been her mistake.

Therefore she pulled herself together and even managed to smile. "Yes. I'll invite you over... as a small compensation."

Sam grinned. "I won't say no to that."

Half an hour later they were sitting comfortably on two small armchairs behind the large window front of the café and - to Katharina's surprise - were engaged in a lively conversation.

She had insisted on giving Sam not only a coffee but also a cupcake and both were now standing between them on the small glass table. Katharina herself had decided to have tea - to calm her tense nerves.

Sam's easy-going manner (she seemed to find the whole thing hilarious after the first thirty seconds) and her relaxed composure soon rubbed off on Katharina, who actually also slowly began to recognise the funny thing about the situation.

Besides, Sam was just incredibly nice and an amusing conversation partner. To relax Katharina, she told her that this was by no means her weirdest Tinder experience.

"I once came unsuspectingly to a date in an ice cream parlour - an ice cream parlour, I emphasise. In a park. With children. And the woman I had a date with turned up completely in leather and lacquer. Including a mask. I'm up for a lot of things, but that was a bit too weird even for me."

She laughed and Katharina had to grin too. She stirred in her tea and shrugged her shoulders. "I once wrote to someone who suggested drinking coffee with his parents as a first date. On Sunday afternoon."

Sam puffed into her coffee. "Either a mega Mama's boy or he wanted to get down to business."

"But why didn't you go? Mothers make great cakes." She bit her cupcake and licked the cream off her upper lip.

Katharina waved away giggling. "I can bake it myself."

Sam teasingly made her eyebrows dance. "Uhhh, wife material..." Then, with a second bite, she destroyed the rest of her cupcake and leaned back in her chair. "So are you really looking for something serious? Well - I mean, not as serious as the coffee party guy..."

"Mmm, yeah, kind of." Katharina shrugged once more and took a sip of her tea. "I'm over 30, I want a family and a house and a yard and all that soon." She blushed slightly. "Boring, I know."

But Sam shook her head violently. "No, not at all... it's nice." Her bright smile left a pleasant feeling in Katharina's stomach.

"And you? Relationship or just adventure?"

Sam tapped the last crumbs from her plate with her finger and then licked it off. For a moment Katharina was spellbound.

"Both, I guess. I just watch what happens. Whoever pretty runs into me." She smiled at Katharina and she blushed again.

Sam laughed gurgling, then suddenly bent forward and with sticky fingertips stroked a strand of hair from Katharina's face. "It's a shame about you... you're just my type." Her voice had become a touch quieter.

Katharina, once again too baffled to react directly, was left sitting there stiff as a post.

Laughing, Sam let herself fall against the back of her chair again. "Don't worry, I won't jump you." She took a sip of her coffee, but then looked at Katharina over the edge of the cup and grinned: "At least I'll try...".

The following conversation became more innocuous again. They talked about Berlin, their jobs, the latest

Disney movies - of which Sam, to Katharina's surprise, was a big fan.

Their cups had long since been empty and all that was left of Sam's cupcake was a practically shiny, licked plate. Outside, the sky had darkened, so the light from the Edison bulbs in the café only shone even warmer. Sam's eyes shimmered almost golden. And Katharina had to admit that she was on a date - even if this was not a date! - she had rarely entertained herself so well.

And so she was almost a little disappointed when Sam now straightened up and pulled her jacket off the back of the chair. "So, shall we go slowly? I don't want to hold you forever." She smiled, almost apologetically.

Katharina, who actually didn't feel held down at all, nodded. "Yes... yes. So..." She turned red again. "Well, it was really very nice..."

Her gaze sank for a moment on the table with the empty cups. She had trouble sorting her thoughts. No, she actually did not want to leave yet. But she could hardly say that, could she? Sam probably had something better to do, too. Or rather, she certainly didn't want to spend the whole afternoon with this non-date that was totally pointless somewhere, when it was already clear that Katharina would not be...

With a jerk she stood up. "I'll pay quickly..." She hurriedly walked over to the counter where a dark-haired waiter was just about to brew some tea. Under other circumstances, she would have noticed how handsome he was, but she paid quickly and her mind was elsewhere.

Sam waited at the front door. "I'm gonna take you to the bus stop, okay?

Katharina just nodded.

They had not gone ten steps when the wind picked up and the first drops of rain fell on the pavement. Sam cursed softly as the rain quickly increased.

"You didn't bring an umbrella either, did you?"

Katharina denied and Sam looked briefly back at the café, then down the street.

"Well, we'd better hurry..."

She already began to run towards the bus stop, pushing the bicycle beside her. Katharina had no other choice but to follow her, even though she made a little more progress in her leather sandals than Sam did in her sneakers.

With a beating heart and completely out of breath she reached the glass bus shelter a little later. Meanwhile it was raining cats and dogs and the smell of wet asphalt hung heavily in the air.

Sam laughed and turned to Katharina and said "All right?"

But she was busy taking a breath and pushed the black hair out of her face. Finally she managed to nod.

Sam's red t-shirt was speckled with water drops and Katharina looked down on herself: she hadn't fared any better - only that her blouse was in danger of becoming transparent in those places. Once again she became a little red.

The next moment she felt Sam's hand rubbing up and down her naked upper arm a few times.

"I hope you don't get cold on the way back..."

Only now did Katharina realise that she had goose bumps. Or had she just got them now? Sam's hand remained on her shoulder for a moment, then she pulled back again. Katharina swallowed.

"In any case, it was a real pleasure to meet you, Katharina." Again Sam smiled in such a way that Katharina got all warm.

"Yeah, you too. And sorry again, about the mix-up..."

Behind her she heard the puffing of the approaching bus.

Sam grinned. "Never mind." Then she suddenly bent over and pressed a little kiss on Katharina's cheek.

It became hot and cold instantly.

Noisily the bus came to a halt in front of them. With a hydraulic hiss the doors opened, two men got out, umbrellas were opened. They moved away hastily. Katharina did not move from the spot.

With another hiss the doors closed again and a moment later the bus started moving.

Silence. Only the sound of the rain.

"Ahem. I think that was your bus."

"Yes." Katharina nodded.

With a beating heart she turned her gaze to Sam. She looked obviously surprised, but then smiled cautiously and took half a step towards Katharina.

"You didn't get on."

"No." The smell of the rain and some fruity scent coming from Sam made Catherine almost dizzy.

Sam's hand lay light as a feather on her cheek, and with her thumb she stroked Katharina's delicate skin. Then she came a little closer.

Their bodies almost touched each other.

Katharina swallowed, opened her lips, wanted to say something and then remained silent. Her gaze hung as if hypnotised in Sam's amber eyes.

Sam's thumb now stroked over her lower lip.

Katharina gasped softly, hardly audible.

The next moment Sam's lips lay on hers - carefully at first, but then with a little more emphasis. Everything around Katharina turned and her eyelids sank down.

Sam tasted like coffee and a little bit of the chocolate of the cupcake. Her lips were softer than any lips Katharina had ever kissed.

She already opened her mouth carefully and sighed softly when Sam's tongue touched her own, circled around her teasingly.

Then she faltered briefly. A little giggle escaped her mouth. What was she doing here?

Sam gurgled, then shoved her hands into Katharina's neck and pulled her gently closer.

Their bodies touched each other. So unfamiliar.

Katharina felt her full breasts nestle slightly against Sam's much flatter breast. Her hands moved to the narrow waist of her, then up her back. She had of course already hugged other women, but this one was completely different.

Sam nibbled slightly on her lower lip, again pushing her tongue between Katherina's lips. Her kiss became more passionate, breathless.

Katharina felt how it began to tingle in her lap. She was dizzy. She could not believe what she was doing here. So new and exciting and... crazy. She wrapped her arms tighter around Sam's waist, squeezing her, gently yet, awkwardly maybe.

Sam's left hand slipped along her neck, forward, over the hem of her blouse. It remained just above her breasts.

Katharina felt how quickly and flatly they lifted themselves under their now more hectic breaths. And she felt that Sam's breath had also become faster.

The hand on her chest seemed to glow.

She stroked Sam's back, felt her spine under the thin t-shirt. Felt Sam shudder in her embrace. Then she gently released from her, just enough to allow a few inches of air between her lips.

"That was a surprise," she whispered.

Katharina, who was now slowly regaining some consciousness, looked at her with big eyes uncertainly. "Yes, I... I don't know..."

"Would you like to come home with me?"

Katharina nodded.

When they arrived at Sam's front door a little later, both were soaked to the skin. Katharina white blouse now stuck half transparent to her curvy body, the light blue lace bra more than just peeking through. Water dripped from Sam's brown hair into her eyes and ran down her high cheekbones.

Laughing, she pushed Katharina into the shelter of her house entrance and then quickly attached her racing bike to a lamppost, before jumping over two puddles, also under the canopy, and digging for her key.

Meanwhile, Katharina still could not quite believe what she was doing. However, she tried not to let doubting thoughts arise and instead concentrated entirely on the present moment.

And it looked like that, so Sam now pressed her gently against the glass of the entrance door and kissed her again.

She gasped for breath. How was it possible that Sam tasted so good? She buried her hands in the short wet hair of the others and shuddered as Sam's tongue seemed to chase tiny little flashes of lightning through her body.

With a small gasp Sam let go of her again, but remained half in the hug while she unlocked the front door with trembling fingers.

Both staggered into the dusky stairwell, where Sam then grabbed Katharina's hand and hurriedly pulled her along. They rumbled up the steps to the second floor.

Another door, another lock.

Sam pulled them into the apartment, pushed the door behind them into the lock and Katharina against it.

She gasped, her heart beat, her cheeks glowed.

Sam's hands stroked her sides, her back, her hips. Her kisses were now faster, more breathless, hungrier.

Katharina herself did not know where to put her hands, her lips. She stroked over all the unknown curves, the wet cloth that covered Sam's sinewy body. She slipped her hands under her T-shirt and only really noticed what she was doing when Sam shuddered with a little sigh and pressed her harder against the apartment door.

Then Sam tore herself away from her, took Katharina's hand again and pulled her with her, down the hall, through a door - the bedroom. A futon bed and long white curtains that moved languidly in the breeze that came from the tilted window. The sound of the rain was a white murmur.

At the sight of the bed Katharina faltered briefly, suddenly insecure again. Was that too fast? Did she really want to?

But Sam was already with her again, took her face in both hands and covered her wet cheeks with kisses.

Katharina trembled and closed her eyes.

She felt Sam stroke her wet hair back, sliding her fingertips over her neck. Sam's lips were back on hers, sweet and full and delicious.

"You should take that off," she whispered into Katharina's mouth. Her fingers carefully opening the first button on her blouse.

Katharina stiffened briefly, but made no attempt to stop Sam.

"Or else you'll get sick..." Sam giggled softly. The second button followed and then the third.

Katharina nodded, even though she hadn't really been listening. She only felt the slender female hands at her neckline, the deft fingers that slid down between her breasts and opened one button after the other.

Then, finally, she peeled the wet cloth from her skin.

The blouse fell to the floor and Katharina shivered.

The next moment Sam had also pulled her own T-shirt over her head.

Unlike Katharina, she did not wear a bra. Her small breasts were naked and tenderly tanned. Her nipples were hard and contracted.

Katharina stared at them with big eyes, let her hands stroke Sam's sides, waist up, completely spellbound. Over the arches of her ribs, which were visible under her skin with every breath she took. She touched the gentle curves of her breasts and Sam trembled and closed her eyes.

Fascinated, Katharina stroked Sam's skin with her fingertips - slowly circling one of the two hard nipples and then carefully, curiously, riding over it.

As Sam gasped, she almost flinched.

Sam opened her eyes again, grabbed Katharina's hands and pulled her towards the bed. In a smooth movement, she let herself sink backwards onto it, pulling Katharina with her, above her.

She couldn't stop looking at Sam's naked torso, admiring it. With her hands propped up, one knee

68

supported between Sam's thighs, she looked down at the foreign woman's body, lifted her right hand and stroked Sam's skin once more. Her décolleté, then through between her breasts, over her flat stomach. She could feel Sam's breaths.

Back up again.

With the whole palm of her hand she rubbed over Sam's left breast, then embraced it briefly. What a strange, delicious feeling. The hard bud pressed itself into her palm.

Sam bent her back and pushed her hand towards Katharina's.

Katharina shivered.

"Use your mouth..." Sam whispered, her voice hushed.

Their glances met briefly, then Katharina followed the invitation - albeit still a little hesitant. Carefully she let her tongue glide over Sam's skin, along her collarbone. Up the hill of her chest. Around the hard bud. Then over it.

Sam moaned.

Katharina, becoming more courageous, closed her lips around the foreign nipple, sucking lightly on it. Played around them with her tongue. She felt Sam tremble beneath her. She herself had closed her eyes now, concentrated only on touching and tasting and feeling. So unfamiliar. So sweet.

Sam's moans were so much brighter than a man's.

Her hands, which now clawed into her back, so much more delicate.

Katharina's body sank down onto Sam's, she felt the one moving under her, her own full breasts pressing against Sam's flat stomach. She nibbled slightly on her right nipple while her hand rubbed over her left and she began to massage the gentle curve. Hesitantly at first, then as Sam made it clear that she liked it, more and more passionately.

Katharina's breath raced.

She groped deeper, covered Sam's flat stomach with tiny kisses and circled her belly button with the tip of her tongue. Reached the waistband of her jeans. There she paused and raised her head, looking for Sam's amber eyes.

She straightened up a little, supported her forearms on the mattress. She nodded, demanding.

Katharina sat up, opened with trembling fingers Sam's jeans wet from the rain. Then pulled them carefully. The pants stuck to the hips, which were much wider than a man's.

Katharina tugged, clumsily, breathlessly, then finally managed to free Sam from her jeans.

Only in socks and panties she now lay in front of her. (She must have kicked the sneakers off her feet earlier.) The slim, muscular thighs. The cotton panties that covered her middle.

Katharina stroked carefully over the light skin, down to the knees. Then up again. Further inside.

Sam sank back into the pillows, opening her thighs with a sigh.

With trembling fingers and a beating heart, Katharina reached for Sam's panties. Pulled again, pushed it down to the back of her knees. Her gaze glided over Sam's shaved vulva, curious, incredulous, admiring. Never before had she seen the naked lap of another woman. So beautiful.

Without really knowing what she was doing, Katharina bent over, touched the tender skin with the tip of her tongue, licked carefully over the labia.

Sam trembled and moaned and opened her thighs a little more with each lick. Her lips parted, wet shimmered the soft pink inside.

Katharina, with held breath and muscles twitching with tension, let her tongue slide deeper, between the swollen lips, into the dark, wonderfully scented interior.

Sam trembled, her hands groped for Catherine's head and she buried her hands in her dark hair.

"Yes... well..." she muttered in a voice breathless with excitement.

The verbal confirmation spurred Katharina on even further, made her more courageous and more inquiring.

Gently she began to let her tongue dance over Sam's vulva. Licking over the wet skin, she pushed herself between the sweet lips. She found the foreign clitoris, circled around it and was amazed at how violently Sam reacted: moaning, she squeezed her back and pressed the pelvis into the mattress.

When Catherine let her tongue slide directly over her pearl, Sam reared up.

"Yes..."

Katharina also felt the excitement bubbling in her loins, how jeans and bra felt much too tight.

She pushed her tongue deeper into Sam's lap, penetrated it easily, tasted all the strange wetness, so unknown and at the same time so intoxicating. Then licked over the pearl again, and again. Faster.

Sam's pelvis twitched. Catherine put her hands on her hips and pressed her onto the bed.

An almost tortured groan was the answer. And Sam's hands clawed harder into her hair.

"Keep going... don't stop..."

Katharina did not even think about quitting. Instead, her play of tongues became even faster, more urgent, more greedy. Her own lap glowed.

Sam moaned, louder and louder, faster and faster. She writhed, pushed herself towards Katharina's tongue. Then her pelvis began to twitch, to cramp. She screamed.

Katharina, completely taken by surprise by what she had triggered, faltered for a moment in her movements.

Moaning, Sam pressed her head into her lap. "Go on!" A harsh, breathless command.

Katharina obeyed, completely overwhelmed by the climax of the woman under her. She felt the cramps that chased through Sam's pelvis under her own lips.

She felt them tremble.

She heard her scream.

Then - slowly - become calmer.

Hands that grabbed Katharina and pulled her up.

Sam's shimmering golden eyes. Her breathless smile. The voice, cooing comfortably. "Not bad... for a first time." A little laugh. "And now it's your turn..."

Wedding Romance

Lilly stared dreamily for a moment at the bouquet of flowers in her hands - cream and white roses - before she turned her gaze back to the bridal couple. A little smile flitted across her freckled face.

Over there her best friend just married her other best friend. She had introduced the two of them to each other almost a year ago and then everything had gone incredibly fast. Hard to believe. Both had wanted her as a maid of honor, but Lilly had given preference to Katharina because they had known each other for a long time - since kindergarten, to be exact.

The wedding ceremony took place outside and they were really lucky with the weather. A mild late summer afternoon, not a cloud in the ink blue sky. The sun shone on the small waves of the lake as well as on the white chairs that had been set up on the shore in the soft grass. The bridal couple under the archway crowned with flowers was a pure postcard motif. Paper flowers and lanterns swayed in the nearby trees, and under the broad branches the tables were waiting for the feast.

Suddenly a whisper sounded in Lilly's right ear.

"I can't believe they're really doing this..."

She turned around and looked into Mark's grinning face.

Katharina's big brother looked even better in his suit than usual. The blond hair fell curly into his forehead, the jacket emphasized his broad shoulders. Despite her light blue evening gown and the dark brown curls perfectly shaped by the hairdresser, Lilly felt just as inadequate at Mark's sight as she had felt when she had secretly adored him at Katharina's birthday party.

She had really had a crush on him for a long time, until one day she realized that big brothers were not interested in their little sister's silly girlfriends.

But in the meantime she was grown up and so she tried not to let her feelings show when she whispered "Shhh" to him with a little smile.

Mark, however, only grinned wider and winked at her briefly before crossing his arms in front of his chest and letting himself fall back into his chair.

Lilly turned back to the front.

But less than thirty seconds later his voice resounded again. "You really did something."

She quickly turned around again and whispered a rebuking, "Mark!" before she briefly put a finger on the red painted lips to finally silence him. At the same time she could not prevent a grin from conjuring up two dimples in her cheeks. It fluttered in her stomach. She looked forward again.

The next moment I felt his breath on her neck. "You look really pretty today, by the way, Lilly." His voice was suddenly no longer mocking at all.

Lilly noticed a small shiver running down her back, but she forced herself not to turn around for him again. A creak told her that he had leaned back again.

Less than half an hour later everything was over. There was fondling and kissing, pressing and congratulating. Petals and confetti swirled through the air. Glasses clinked. Lilly sipped her champagne and with her free hand plucked a few pieces of confetti from her chin-length curls. She watched her friends with a smile, but also a little melancholy.

Suddenly Mark was next to her again, gently clinking his glass against hers and then taking a sip, also looking at the bridal couple surrounded by friends.

"My little sister..." Almost incredulous, he shook his head, but then turned back to Lilly with a beaming smile. "Shall we jump on the buffet while the others are still distracted?"

Lilly hesitated for a moment and looked over to the tables under the trees, where two caterers were already pulling the lids off the first bowls and dishes.

Then she glanced back at her friends, shrugged her narrow shoulders and gave Mark a smile.

"Sure, why not?"

But just as they were about to leave the group, they were stopped by one of the two photographers hired for the wedding. The black-haired man in his forties smiled at them with a challenge.

"A photo?"

It was more a challenge than a question. Lilly, who did not like to be photographed, was about to refuse when Mark jovially nodded. "Sure thing."

The photographer, obviously very satisfied, waved his hands in the air. "All right! Then a little closer together please!"

Lilly - herself stiff as a poker - felt Mark put his arm around her shoulders without hesitation. Her heart made a few uncontrolled jumps and her knees became soft. His aftershave rose into her nose. She felt his hand on her naked upper arm burning hot. It flashed and Lilly blinked irritated. Had she smiled at all?

"Enchanting," the photographer said enthusiastically. "They are a wonderful couple".

Lilly would have loved to sink into the ground.

But Mark just laughed, "Now let's go eat - before the best is gone.

Together they walked over the grass to the buffet and Lilly was happy that she had chosen ballerinas instead of pumps - even if it meant that Mark outdid her by more than a head.

The food smelled tempting and while they were filling their plates, Lilly - who had helped Katharina with the preparations - explained that the food came from their favorite vegan restaurant.

"But the cupcakes are from a café in Kreuzberg," she added and carefully placed one of the pink decorated cupcakes on her plate.

"Cute," smiled Mark. "Cute cupcakes for cute girls."

He winked at her. Before Lilly could say anything back, he offered her his arm in the next moment and pointed to the blackboard with the fully loaded plate. "I guess you're my dinner partner anyway."

Yeah, that's right. And Lilly would have to be lying if she claimed that she hadn't had a hand in that.

She gently pushed her narrow right hand into Mark's crook of his arm and let him lead her to the table decorated with flowers and candles.

The other guests followed them a little later and shortly after that the banquet was in full swing. Voices flirted like mosquitoes in the warm summer air, now and then a glass clinked and a short speech interrupted the feast.

But Lilly had almost only eyes for Mark. Already during the meal they talked animatedly and even when their plates were long empty in front of them, they remained seated together.

The golden sun over the lake slowly sank deeper, first fairy lights and lanterns began to sparkle in the branches. Lilly was amazed by the attention Mark suddenly gave her - she didn't believe she had ever talked to him for so long before. And he seemed to really listen to her: His dark blue gaze lay on her with a concentrated intensity that made her almost dizzy and made her feel, more than once, that she was blushing under his piercing gaze.

Suddenly music blew through the evening air and Mark paused. Lilly also looked up. Most of the guests were now cavorting on the temporary dance floor that had been set up on the lakeside, where the bridal couple was just starting to make their first circles.

Smiling, Mark tilted his head to the side and looked at Lilly questioningly. "Do you want to dance?"

She blinked in surprise for a moment and then smiled at him radiantly. "I'd love to."

Again he offered her his arm and she hooked underneath - a movement that felt almost familiar now.

No sooner had they reached the dance floor than he gently grabbed her hand with his left and let his right slide to her waist. She felt his touch through the thin fabric of her blue dress.

Mark was a good dancer and led them gently but firmly. Lilly, who was afraid for a moment of being too clumsy, found that she glided across the floor in his arms almost effortlessly. And she enjoyed it! She laughed gurgling as he whirled her around and Mark grinned contentedly.

Shortly after, the music calmed down a bit and Mark pulled her closer into his arms. Lilly noticed her heart beating faster again. Through the fabric of his jacket she felt Mark's muscular shoulder under her left hand.

Carefully, she nestled a little closer to his chest, feeling his grip around her waist tighten as well. Her head now rested on his shoulder, the smell of his aftershave enveloped her. Lilly even believed to hear his heartbeat. Almost completely at rest, they now swayed slowly back and forth. Lilly had completely forgotten the other guests and dancers.

Mark's right hand on her back slid a little higher, reaching the edge of her low-cut dress at the back and touching the soft skin above. Slowly he stroked her spine with his fingertips and Lilly shivered. She felt that her nipples were getting hard, and was glad that he could hardly notice that - as tight as she was snuggling up to him.

His hand reached her neck, briefly gripped her throat - Lilly stopped breathing for a moment - and then slid back down the same path, chasing another shiver through her body. This time his movement ended a little further down than it had begun: instead of at her waist, his hand came to rest on her tailbone, almost as if he was pressing her pelvis lightly against his own.

Lilly hardly dared to move - her left hand alone clawed slightly into the fabric of his jacket. She did not know when she had closed her eyes.

"Lilly..."

Mark's voice was a harsh whisper in her ear, echoing darkly in her and making her swallow dry. His thumb stroked lightly over the side of her index finger.

She blinked, didn't want to move at first, and then dared to do so: carefully, she detached herself from him just far enough so that she could put her head back into his neck and raise her gaze to him.

The grin that had dominated his facial features all evening had disappeared. Instead, his blue eyes now shimmered darkly and there was something almost desperate about his gaze.

Lilly's own brown eyes widened a little, briefly opening her full lips to say something, but then not knowing what, she closed them again. For a moment they only looked at each other - one caught in the gaze of the other. Only after a few seconds delay did Lilly realize that they were no longer dancing, but had stopped.

Suddenly Mark blinked as if he was waking up from a dream (or a very complicated thought). He lifted his eyes, looked around briefly and then looked back down at Lilly.

"A little walk?"

This time he not only dispensed with a complete movement, but also with any grin or playful head wryness.

Lilly, still completely spellbound by him, just nodded.

But Mark seemed to have hardly waited for her answer, and then he grabbed her hand and almost hurriedly pulled her through the turmoil of the wedding guests, who had long since started dancing more lively again. They had just left the circle of light on the dance floor when Catherine's voice sounded behind her back:

"All single ladies to the front, please. Time for the bridal bouquet!"

Under the trees that surrounded the festival meadow it was dusky, almost gloomy. But the dull darkness was enchanted by the fairy lights and lanterns that sparkled throughout the branches. There was a smell of moss, resin, and very slightly of the flowers of the wedding decorations.

Mark was still dragging Lilly behind him, even though his steps were not quite as hasty now. But only when they had entered a good ten metres into the forest and the happy voices of the wedding party had become a little quieter, he finally stopped and turned to her.

The next moment Lilly felt his hands on her cheeks and then his lips on hers. Surprised, she gasped up. His hands slipped across her neck onto her back and now it was her who in turn wrapped her arms around his neck and returned the kiss.

He grabbed her tighter, pulled her to himself.

Lilly opened her mouth slightly and tasted his tongue, felt her teasingly stroking around her own.

Her breath went faster, she sighed at his lips and heard him growl softly.

Mark quickly pushed it two steps backwards until it hit a tree trunk, against which he only pressed it harder the next moment.

"If you only knew... how long I... wanted to... do this...", Lilly heard him murmur softly into the kiss, while his hands stroked her sides, her shoulders, her bare upper arms.

Everything in her was tingling and glowing, she buried her hands in his blond curls, looking for a hold. She couldn't believe what was happening here, she couldn't believe how good he tasted, how soft his lips were. How his shoulders felt and his chest. His smell made her dizzy. She never thought Mark would ever kiss her like that. That he would ever kiss her.

But now he was here and his hands clawed into the silky fabric of her dress.

"Mark," she whispered.

"Lilly...", he answered and gently bit her lower lip.

Then he almost tore himself away from her lips - only to let his mouth slide over her cheek to her neck. A trail of hasty kisses, down her neck, to her shoulder. Meanwhile, his left hand glided up, stroking the curve of her shoulder and reaching the narrow strap of her dress.

He had already pushed it over her shoulder and Lilly felt the neckline of her dress slip - and slipped even more when she let her hands slide from his neck to his chest.

Mark's kisses wandered further, over her collarbone and deeper down. His tongue stroked her delicate skin, reaching the upper base of her chest. He had now gripped the fabric of her dress tighter, pulled on it and freed the left breast from its textile prison.

Lilly sucked in the air with a sigh as his breath brushed over her naked skin and her nipple only tightened more.

The next moment Mark's lips closed around her nipple.

Lilly moaned.

He also gasped, pressing her more firmly against the tree, his pelvis against hers.

The rough bark of the tree pressed itself painfully into her back, but she hardly felt it.

While Mark's tongue circled her nipple and sent sweet, hot shivers through Lilly's body, her hands clawed into the fabric of his shirt, seeking a hold.

Suddenly he grabbed her by the waist and lifted her up with a jerk. Lilly immediately wrapped her slender legs around his hips, causing her dress to slide up to the middle of her thighs. His hands were now also on her thighs and greedily he pushed her skirt a little further up.

Lilly could now clearly feel Mark's excitement between her thighs. And even her own could hardly be hidden anymore.

He had now also exposed her other breast, and his lips, his tongue, elicited one lustful sigh after another. A bite into her right nipple made her groan.

But Mark wasn't satisfied with her breasts - he already pushed his pelvis harder against hers and Lilly felt his hard manhood rubbing against her pussy through the fabric of his pants. She gasped for breath.

The tingling and throbbing in her lap was already almost unbearable, she longed to feel it, to feel it within her.

He rubbed himself harder against her, clawed his hands into her buttocks. The fabric of her dress rushed. From the festival meadow laughter broke over.

Lilly's lips were now on Mark's ear, she nibbled his earlobe briefly - he moaned - then she whispered softly, hoarse: "Take me...Now...".

He groaned, almost growled. He couldn't be asked twice: he had already opened his trousers with his right hand, then pushed his hand under the skirt of her dress that had slid up and between her legs to grab her panties with his deft fingers.

One piece of advice and he had torn the thin cloth - torn away.

Lilly gasped.

In the next moment, he penetrated her with a single powerful movement.

Only the crook of his neck dampened Lilly's lustful outcry.

He filled her, great and mighty.

She had hardly gotten used to the intoxicating feeling when he had already begun to move inside her, driving her up with smooth strokes against and along the trunk.

Lilly, panting, groaning, slung her arms around his neck, looking for a hold. Her lap took him, hot and greedy. With each in or out, the shaft of his cock rubbed against her sensitive pearl, chasing hot flashes of pure lust through her quivering body.

Soon her head sank into the neck, her moans mingled with the cheerful noise that blew over from the wedding.

But Lilly had long forgotten where she was, only she and Mark existed in the world, she and he and the hard tree trunk in her back.

The more she forgot herself, the harder and deeper he pushed into her, the louder her moaning, panting and sighing became. Mark's right hand was already resting on her mouth, dampening the sounds of lust that were bubbling from her lips.

She blinked into the blackness of the treetop, glittering with thousands of dots of light, then looked into Mark's smiling face, which briefly whispered a gentle "Shh" to her, but the next moment looked at her so hungry that she knew that he really just wanted to make her scream louder.

Hard and demanding, he poked into her lap, glowing and red the excitement bubbling in her body.

The hand that he now pressed firmly on her lips took her breath away and - instead of frightening her - made her even dizzier. Her screams, now only a muffled groan, her eyelids half lowered, hardly able to keep the dancing lights around her apart.

Suddenly, however, he slowed down, then paused.

Tormented, she groaned and writhed in his arms.

He just held it even tighter.

Fluttering, Lilly opened her eyes again and met Mark's gaze. Dark, hungry. Obviously drunk at the sight of the excitement on her face.

He moved a little inside her - Lilly closed her eyes moaning.

Then he paused again.

The sizzling heat was like an agonising itch that only his blows could soothe. If he denied it to her, she thought she could hardly bear the excitement any longer. Angrily, she tried to bite his hand, which he still pressed firmly to her lips.

Mark laughed, softly, darkly. Pressed his fingers only more firmly on her mouth.

Then he pulled his tail away from her - agonisingly slowly - and let her glide gently to the ground the next moment. Lilly whimpered. She had lost her ballerinas long ago, and she felt wet moss and leaves under her bare feet.

The next moment Mark had her twirling around, one hand on her hip, the other now on her shoulder - gently pushing her forward, down. Lilly's trembling hands found a hold on the rough bark of the tree trunk.

Rustling, Mark pushed the fabric of her dress up her bottom. His rough voice at her ear. "I don't have a condom..."

Then his tail, which was wet, pressed slipperily against the firmly closed rosette of her anus.

Lilly gasped, but less from surprise than from excitement. She would have let him do anything at that moment if she could only feel him inside her.

Already he increased the pressure, only laboriously defeated urge. The tip of his tail squeezed into her ass, stretching her painfully & excitably.

Lilly whimpered. The next moment she felt his arm, which was wrapped around her hip, his hand, which was pushed from the front under her skirt and between her thighs. With two fingers he parted her slippery wet lips, rubbing gently over her clitoris. She moaned. Relaxed. His tail pushed deeper, slipping into her inch by inch.

She heard Mark moaning behind her, breathless. His arms trembled, his muscles tensed to the point of tearing. She could feel how painstakingly he controlled himself, how much he just wanted to push into her with a jerk.

Instead, he forced himself to slow down, but in return he now penetrated her lap with two fingers. Groaning, Lilly's upper body sank deeper down, her hands gliding over the rough bark of the tree trunk, seeking a hold. Through the black silhouettes of the trees, she saw colorfully dressed figures fluttering around in the distance like butterflies. Music and laughter. Her body a single ball of fire.

His cock inside her now felt twice as big as before in her vagina - he seemed to want to tear her apart. The pressure almost brought the heat inside her to boiling point.

The two fingers were joined by a third. At the same time Mark slid into her anus with a last small jerk until it stopped.

Lilly gasped. Could hardly keep still and moved her pelvis, only slightly, small circles. Sweat glittered on her naked skin.

Mark fucked her now simultaneously with his cock and fingers, first slowly, then rapidly becoming faster. His palm rubbed over her clitoris.

When Lilly's moans became louder again, his other hand found its way back to her mouth, lying heavily on her lips. Trembling, Lilly closed her eyes.

Soon they moved in a joyful rhythm, back and forth, back and forth. A different kind of dance - much more animalistic than before. Lilly's full naked breasts - now completely freed from her dress - swung with every movement.

Mark growled in her back, groaned when he sank his tail again deep into her now slippery, stretched anus.

Lilly screamed muffled under the ever faster playing of his fingers.

Harder and deeper he pushed into it, faster and more urgently his fingers moved.

Her pelvis twitched, her heart seemed to want to roll over.

Lights and music and shadows and his hand on her mouth.

Above and below lost themselves in a staggering stupor.

Even harder, even deeper.

Her muscles began to cramp.

Likewise his own.

He grabbed her tighter, moaning her name on her ear.

Pushed her butt once more, pressed her on his pelvis.

Lilly felt his cock pumping inside her, twitching.

At the same time he rubbed hard over her clitoris, pressing the ball of his hand on her mons veneris.

The orgasm almost tore her off her feet.

Even his hand on her mouth could hardly muffle her screams.

Her legs gave way to it, only her arms and the trunk still held her upright. At the same time, the twitching waves of the climax threw her forward, back, away from him, into his embrace.

She gasped for breath - his hand on her mouth.

Dancing lights, then she saw black before her eyes.

Or had she just closed her eyes?

Twitching, cramping, raging heat.

When Lilly came to slowly and heavily breathing, they both lay on the mossy forest floor. Above them the lanterns danced in the now inky black darkness of the night. She lay on her side, in Mark's arms, her head resting on his shoulders. Her lap was still glowing in a delicious aftershock.

His fingers gently brushed some sweaty curls from her face. Then his hand slid deeper, between her breasts, over her flat stomach and between her thighs. For a moment his fingers parted her still wet labia and stroked her sensitive pearl. Lilly moaned with a sweet shiver, then she quietly pushed Mark's hand aside in protest and rolled over on her back.

He laughed and bent over her.

For a moment their two glances met, then he breathed a brief kiss on her lips before muttering softly: "I've been wanting to do that for a very long time..."

9 798841 261551